DILYS PRICE

NORMAN
PRICE

BELLA
LASAGNE

JAMES

SARAH

MEET ALL THESE FRIENDS IN BUZZ BOOKS:

Thomas the Tank Engine
Fireman Sam
Looney Tunes
Tiny Toon Adventures
Bugs Bunny
Toucan 'Tecs
Flintstones
Jetsons
Joshua Jones

First published by Buzz Books,
an imprint of Reed Consumer Books Ltd
Michelin House, 81 Fulham Road, London SW3 6RB

LONDON MELBOURNE AUCKLAND

Fireman Sam © copyright 1985 Prism Art & Design Ltd
Text © copyright 1992 William Heinemann Ltd
Illustrations © copyright 1992 William Heinemann Ltd
Based on the animation series produced by Bumper Films
for S4C/Channel 4 Wales and Prism Art & Design Ltd
Original idea by Dave Gingell and Dave Jones,
assisted by Mike Young. Characters created by Rob Lee.
All rights reserved.

ISBN 1 85591 251 1

Printed and bound in the UK by BPCC Hazell Books Ltd

SEASIDE ADVENTURE

Story by Rob Lee
Illustrations by The County Studio

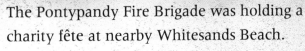

The Pontypandy Fire Brigade was holding a charity fête at nearby Whitesands Beach.

"It's jolly good of the Newtown Fire Brigade to be on call at Pontypandy today," said Fireman Sam.

"And to give me time off for the fête," added Firefighter Penny Morris.

Trevor Evans gazed hungrily at Sam's cakes. "Should I have a chocolate éclair, a slice of fruit cake or a gingerbread man?" he asked. "I know! I'll have one of each."

"At this rate we'll make a fortune for the Pontypandy Children's Hospital," chuckled Fireman Sam.

Norman, James and Sarah raced onto the beach with their buckets and spades.

"Let's build a giant sandcastle!" Norman shouted excitedly.

"I'd rather collect shells," said James.

"Yes, we can give the shells to Penny for her crafts stall," Sarah suggested.

"You two go on," said Norman. "I'm going to build the best sandcastle in the universe!"

As Norman filled his bucket with sand, the twins searched for shells.

"There aren't many shells on the beach today," said James gloomily.

"Look!" said Sarah. "There's a cave in the cliffs. I bet there are lots of shells in there. Let's go and see."

The twins raced across the sand to the cave and peered inside.

"I don't think we should go in there," said James nervously. "It could be haunted."

"Don't be a scaredy cat," chuckled Sarah. "Come on, let's explore."

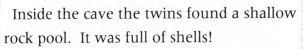

Inside the cave the twins found a shallow rock pool. It was full of shells!

"Brill!" cried Sarah, her voice echoing as she paddled into the crystal clear water.

"Look at all the shells," said James excitedly. "Loads of them!"

On the promenade Station Officer Steele served Dilys a glass of cool punch.

"Perfect for a hot day like today, don't you think?" he said.

"Oh yes, very nice," Dilys agreed.

Station Officer Steele rattled his bucket. "Aren't you forgetting something, Dilys?"

"Silly me," clucked Dilys, dropping some change into the bucket. "I always like to give to a good cause."

"I have only one cake left," said Sam. "Would you like it, Station Officer Steele?"

"I don't normally approve of sweets, you know," said Station Officer Steele. "But as it's for charity, I don't mind if I do."

"I might as well close up the stall as I've no cakes left to sell," said Fireman Sam.

"Yes, why don't you relax on the beach for a bit, Sam," Station Officer Steele said generously. "You've done a good job."

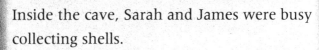

Inside the cave, Sarah and James were busy
collecting shells.

"My bucket's almost full," said James,
placing another shell carefully on the top.

"Shh," said Sarah. She held a large shell to
her ear. "I think I can hear the sea."

"No wonder!" cried James. "The tide is
coming in!"

"The water is rising fast!" exclaimed Sarah. "James, how are we going to get back to the beach?"

"I don't know," said James. "Come on, let's climb onto that ledge."

Quickly, the twins clambered onto the ledge as the water poured through the cave entrance.

Nearby Norman was putting the finishing touches on his sandcastle.

"The biggest, most fantastic sandcastle ever built!" boasted Norman proudly as he stood back to admire his handiwork.

Suddenly, he heard a faint shout, "Help!" Another voice shouted, "We're stuck!"

Norman recognised the voices. "That sounds like the twins!" he thought.

He headed towards the cave, but it was now cut off entirely from the beach by the incoming tide.

"Oh no!" he gasped. "Sarah and James are trapped! I must get help."

Norman raced down the beach as fast as he could until he reached Fireman Sam.

"Fireman Sam, you've got to help!" cried Norman.

"Great fires of London!" Sam exclaimed
when Norman had told him the problem.
He dashed down the beach to the jetty.

"Station Officer Steele, I need your help,"
Sam told him. "We'll have to commandeer
one of these boats."

As Fireman Sam and Station Officer Steele untied a speedboat, Sam quickly explained the situation. A moment later, they were roaring off towards the cave.

"Hurry, Fireman Sam," Station Officer Steele said grimly. "The tide is still rising."

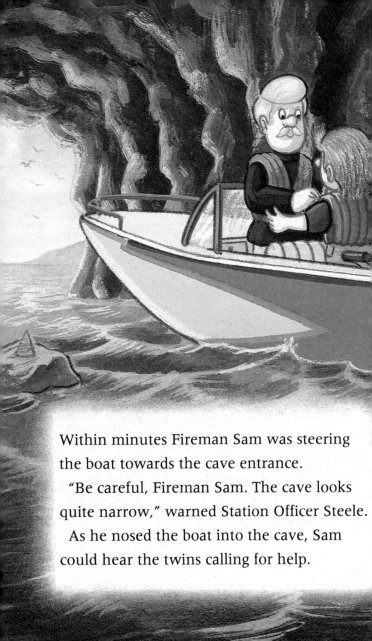

Within minutes Fireman Sam was steering the boat towards the cave entrance.

"Be careful, Fireman Sam. The cave looks quite narrow," warned Station Officer Steele.

As he nosed the boat into the cave, Sam could hear the twins calling for help.

"Stay calm!" he called. "Help is on the way."

"Hurray, we're saved!" shouted Sarah and James as they caught sight of the boat.

Fireman Sam pulled up alongside the ledge. "Steady," he said as the twins climbed aboard. "We don't want you falling in the water."

The children laughed as the speedboat raced across the sea towards the jetty.

"This is brill!" giggled Sarah, her hair whipping about in the wind.

Just then, however, the boat began to cough and splutter.

Sam glanced at the controls. "That's done it," he groaned. "We're out of petrol."

On the promenade, Norman spotted the floundering speedboat. "Something's wrong with Fireman Sam's boat!" he cried.

"You're right. It looks as if he's got engine trouble," said Penny, springing into action. "Elvis, you row out to the speedboat with Venus's lifeline. I'll start unwinding it."

Fireman Sam and Station Officer Steele
tried paddling the speedboat with their
hands, but it was no use.

"I'm afraid we're just going around in
circles, Sir," panted Fireman Sam.

"Look!" cried James. "There's Elvis!"

Fireman Sam gave a sigh of relief at the
sight of Elvis in the little dinghy, doggedly
rowing against the tide to reach them.

"Good work, Cridlington!" beamed Station
Officer Steele as Elvis climbed into the
speedboat with the lifeline.

"Er, thank you, Sir," replied Elvis proudly.

Elvis secured the dinghy to the back of the
speedboat while Station Officer Steele
attached the lifeline to the front.

Penny watched from inside Venus's cab.
When she saw Station Officer Steele give the
signal, she started the engine and pressed the
rewind button on the winch.

"I do like a relaxing boat ride," said Elvis, as
the boats were slowly towed towards shore.

"Look! So does that bird," chuckled James.

27

"You could have spent a cold night in that cave if it hadn't been for Norman's prompt action," Fireman Sam told James and Sarah when they were safely on shore.

"Thank you, Norman," said the twins.

Sam placed a plastic firefighter's helmet on Norman's head.

"For your help today, I name you an honorary firefighter," said Sam.

Everyone clapped.

"Magic! Thanks, Fireman Sam." Norman picked up his bucket and spade. "Now that I'm a firefighter, I'd better build myself a fire station!"

FIREMAN SAM

STATION OFFICER
STEELE

TREVOR EVANS

ELVIS
CRIDLINGTON

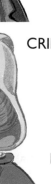

PENNY MORRIS